Little Bear's Little Boat

by Eve Bunting

Illustrated by Nancy Carpenter

BLOOMSBURY
CHILDREN'S
BOOKS

First published in Great Britain in 2004 by Bloomsbury Publishing Plc
38 Soho Square, London, W1D 3HB

First published in America by Clarion Books
a Houghton Mifflin Company imprint
215 Park Avenue South, New York, NY 10003

A CIP catalogue record of this book is available from the British Library

ISBN 0 7475 7478 2

Printed in Hong Kong/China

3 5 7 9 10 8 6 4 2

All papers used by Bloomsbury Publishing are natural, recyclable products made
from wood grown in well-managed forests. The manufacturing processes conform to
the environmental regulations of the country of origin.

For Tracy and Glenn's new little bear, with Grandma's love
—E.B.

For Quin, for taking care of my little bear
—N.C.

Little Bear loved his little boat.

He rowed it all around Huckleberry Lake.

He fished from it.

On sunny days he lay back in it, closed his eyes, and dreamed. And he was happy.

When his mother called him in for bed, he
pulled his little boat up to the shore.

"Good night, little boat," he said. "I'll see you
tomorrow." And he always did.

But then something happened.

Little Bear began to grow and grow.

He got **bigger**

and **bigger**.

Soon he was not a little bear any more.
He was a **BIG BEAR**.
And he didn't fit in his little boat.

He tried to sit in it as it bobbed on the lake.
But he and the little boat both sank down,
down to the bottom of the blue, blue water.

"Where are you, my big bear?" Mother called.

Big Bear and his little boat both spluttered up.

"Glug!" Big Bear said.

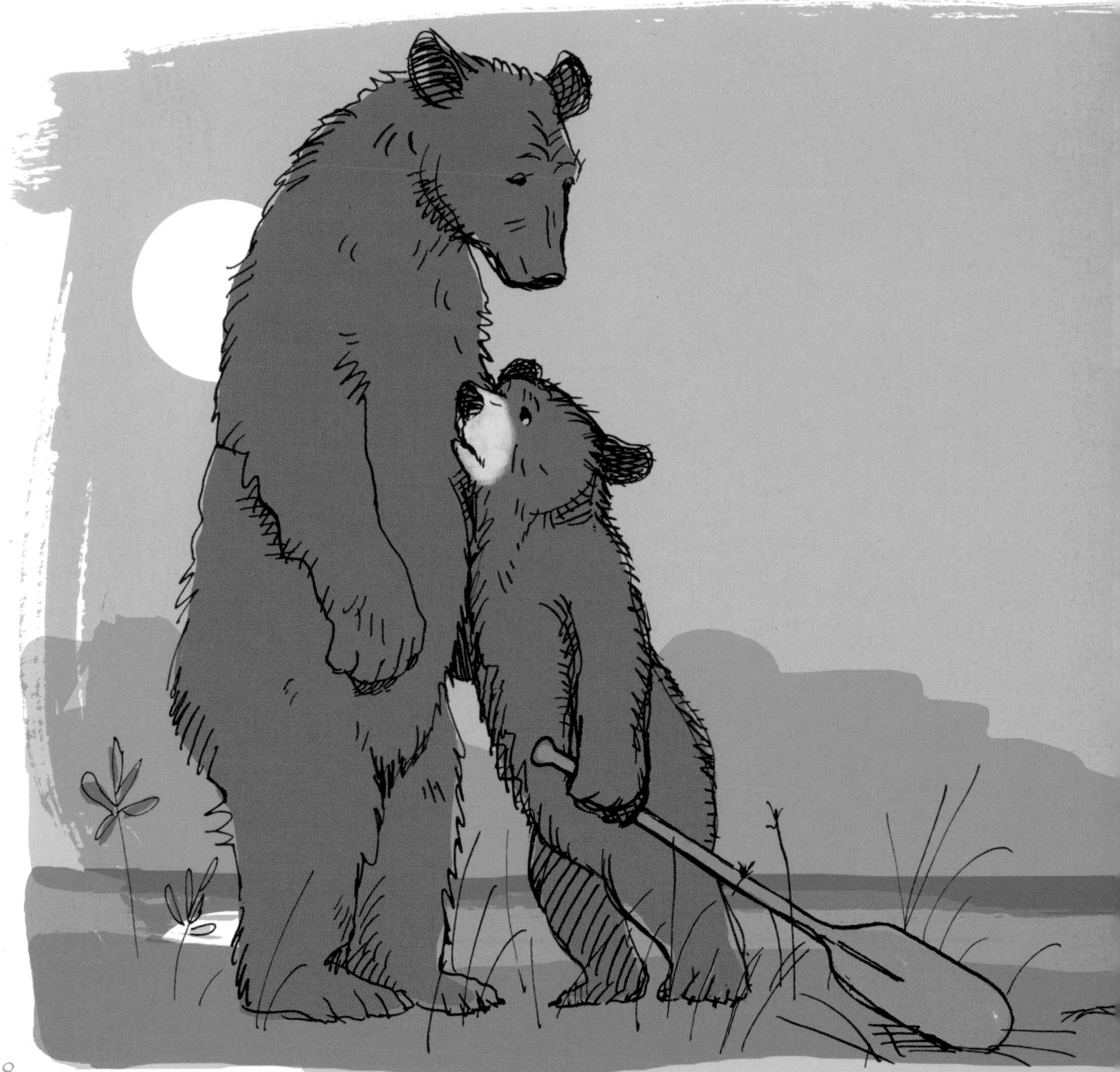

"You are too big a bear now to fit in that little boat," Mother said. "It is a little bear's destiny to grow and grow till he is a BIG BEAR. It is a little boat's destiny to stay the same size."

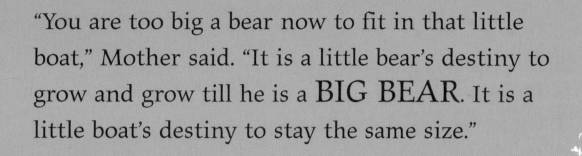

Big Bear was sad.

"I can't leave my little boat with no bear to sit in it, or fish from it, or dream in it," he said. "It is a little boat's destiny to keep sailing on a blue, blue lake."

He scratched his head. "I know! I will find another little bear who will love my little boat the way I love it."

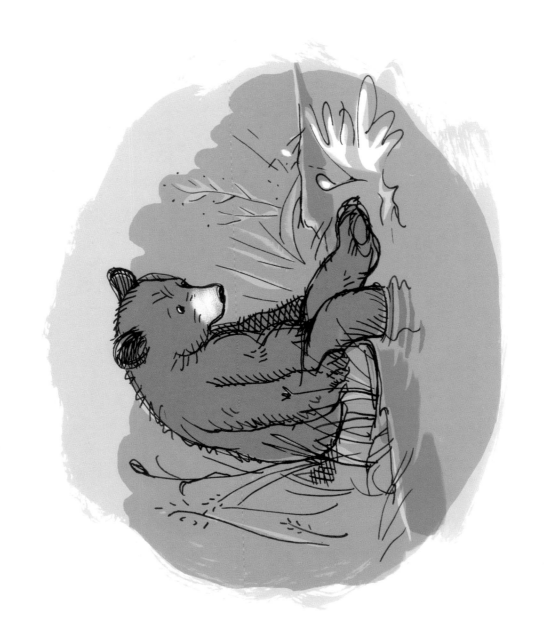

Big Bear walked around Huckleberry Lake.

"Have you seen any little bears anywhere?" he asked Beaver.

"Not since you were a little bear yourself," Beaver said.

Otter hadn't seen a little bear, either.

But Blue Heron had.

"One lives with his mother on the other side of the lake," he said. "I saw him eating berries this very morning."

So Big Bear walked around the lake again and found the little bear.

"I have a little boat for you," Big Bear said. "But there is one thing you should know. You will get bigger and **bigger** till you are a BIG BEAR. That is a little bear's destiny."

The little bear listened carefully.

"The little boat will stay the same size because that is *its* destiny. When that happens, you must find another little bear to fit in the little boat. Because it is also a little boat's destiny to keep sailing on a blue, blue lake. Will you promise?"

"I promise," the little bear said.

All summer long Big Bear saw the little bear
rowing the little boat around Huckleberry Lake.

And fishing from it.

And on sunny days Big Bear would stop what he was doing and watch the little bear as he lay back in the little boat, dreaming. Big Bear could tell that the little bear was happy.

Big Bear was happy, too.